W9-AZL-003

NOT FOR RESALE
This is a Free Book
Bookthing.org

DISCARD

A DARK DARK TALE

For William, Edward and Alice Cowling

J E
Bro

J-107,609

Copyright © 1981 by Ruth Brown
All rights reserved.
First published in Great Britain
by Andersen Press Ltd.
Printed in Great Britain
First U.S.A. printing

Library of Congress Cataloging in Publication Data
Brown, Ruth. A dark dark tale.
Summary: Journeying through a dark, dark house,
a black cat surprises the only inhabitant
of the abandoned residence.
[1. Dwellings—Fiction. 2. Cats—Fiction.
3. Mice—Fiction] I. Title. II. Series.
PZ7.B81698Dar 1981   [E]   81-66798
ISBN 0-8037-1672-9   AACR2
ISBN 0-8037-1673-7 (lib. bdg.)

The art consists of acrylic paintings that are
camera-separated and reproduced in full color.

A DARK DARK TALE

Story and pictures by

RUTH BROWN

 The Dial Press / New York

Once upon a time there
was a dark, dark moor.

On the moor there was
a dark, dark wood.

**In the wood there was
a dark, dark house.**

At the front of the house
there was a dark, dark door.

Behind the door there
was a dark, dark hall.

In the hall there were
some dark, dark stairs.

Up the stairs there was
a dark, dark passage.

**Across the passage was
a dark, dark curtain.**

Behind the curtain was
a dark, dark room.

In the room was a dark,
dark cupboard.

In the cupboard was
a dark, dark corner.

In the corner was
a dark, dark box.

And in the box there was ... A MOUSE!

RUTH BROWN
studied art at the Birmingham College of Art and the Royal College of
Art. She has worked on animated films for the BBC and is the author
of one previous children's book, *Crazy Charlie.*

Ms. Brown lives in London with her husband and two sons.

COLLINGSWOOD FREE PUBLIC LIBRARY
JE   jE Bro   J-107,609
Brown, Ruth. A dark, dark tale :

3 6431 0002 1183 4